CHADWICK
THE
CRAB

By
Priscilla Cummings

Illustrated by A.R.Cohen

Tidewater Publishers
Centreville, Maryland

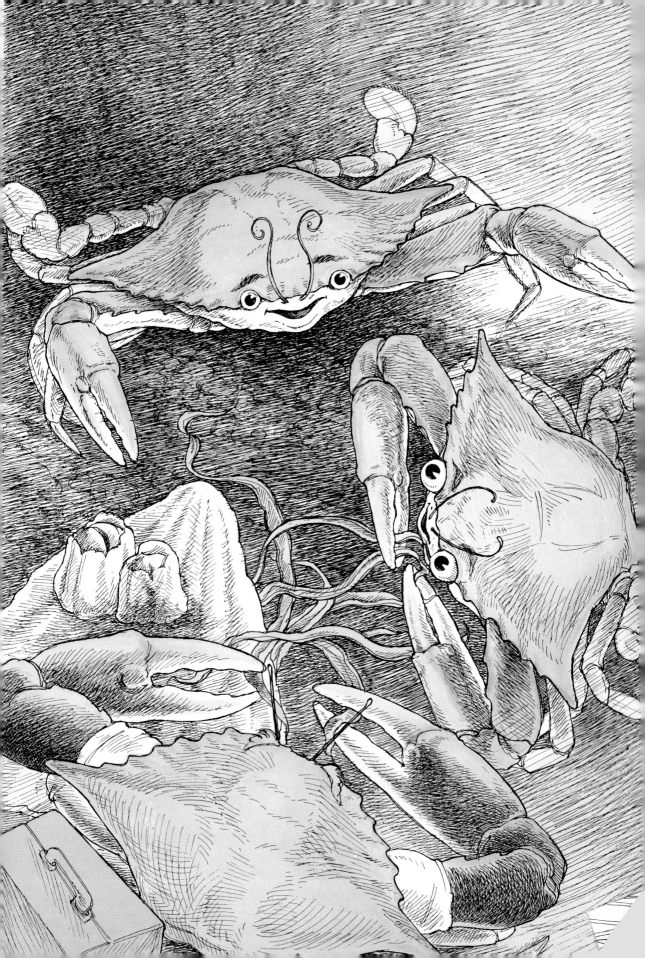

Beneath the deep, blue waters of the Chesapeake Bay, where sailboats skim over the waves and fishermen fish, there lived a crab named Chadwick.

Chadwick was not a very large crab, but he could swim faster than any of his buddies and he was *quite* handsome. His shell was greenish brown, but he was called a blue crab for the stripe of bright blue color that ran down his thick claws.

Chadwick liked to have fun and though he had lots of friends, he worried that there was more to life than eating eel grass and playing games in the marsh. He yearned for an adventure—for fame and fortune! And he was beginning to wonder if others felt the same way.

"Is there something missing in your life?" Chadwick asked Bug-Eyed Benny, a crab whose eyes seemed to pop right out of his head.

"Well, no," said Bug-Eyed Benny. "Not that I can see."

Chadwick asked Pincher Pete, a crab who had claws so strong he could squeeze a tin can in half. "Is there something you could use in your life, Pete?"

"Why, yes," Pete said. "A new suitcase."

"A suitcase?" Chadwick looked confused.

"Yes," said Pete. "For the trip to the bottom of the bay this winter."

Chadwick's eyes drooped. It was fall, time for the crabs to start packing for their annual trip to the deep and warmer water at the bottom of the bay where they spent the cold, winter months napping. It was something Chadwick did not enjoy. He hated to admit it, but it was terribly boring.

Chadwick didn't want to think about the winter nap so he drifted off in the water and headed for Shady Creek to find his friend, Orville the Oyster. Chadwick liked to talk to Orville—even if Orville never talked back. Orville just stayed in his shell, day in and day out. He never went anywhere and he never did anything. But Chadwick had a hunch Orville was always listening and was really very smart.

Before Chadwick could say anything to Orville though, Matilda burst through the tall marsh grass and tripped over the oyster.

"Oh, good afternoon, young crab," she said in her shrill voice as she straightened her pillbox hat. Matilda was a fussy old egret, who wore reading glasses halfway down her beak because her eyes were so bad. She was always squinting and bumping into things. This embarrassed her because Matilda was a very polite and proper bird. Why, she didn't even like to get her feet wet and when she walked through the marsh she picked her dainty, long legs high up out of the water.

"Hello, Matilda," said Chadwick. "How are you?"

"I'm fine. But these oysters," she grumped. "Don't they have anything better to do than just lie around in the sand?" She ruffled her feathers angrily and strutted off in a huff.

Chadwick chuckled and dug his little legs into the cool sand. He thought about taking a trip—maybe going to visit his Uncle Fred, a fiddler crab who lived in a marsh off the North Carolina coast. But North Carolina was a long way from Maryland, too far for a Chesapeake Bay blue crab to swim.

A rustling in the bushes startled Chadwick.

"Ah, bonjour!" a voice called out.

It was Toulouse, the French Canada goose. Toulouse had taught Chadwick several words in French. "Bonjour" meant "hello."

"Hello—I mean bonjour," Chadwick said, but without his usual cheerfulness. Seeing Toulouse only reminded Chadwick that it was autumn, the time of year when the French Canada geese arrived from the north to vacation for the winter. And autumn just wasn't a very happy time for Chadwick.

"Ah, but what is wrong with my little friend?" Toulouse asked. "You are sad today, no?"

"I am a little depressed," said Chadwick. "I think what I need is some excitement in my life." He sighed. "Toulouse, what are *you* going to do this winter?"

"Well," said Toulouse, smiling. "Funny you should ask. I'm going to open a French cooking school on the Eastern Shore."

"Oh, Toulouse! How exciting! May I help?" Chadwick jumped up out of the sand. "With all my claws and legs I'd be a big help in the kitchen!"

Toulouse thought about that for a moment, but then shook his head slowly. "I'm afraid that would not work out, my little friend."

"Oh, but why?" Chadwick wanted to know.

Toulouse rubbed his beak with one wing, wondering how to tell Chadwick without hurting the crab's feelings. "Well, the cooking school is going to be in a cornfield, and I think this would be a problem for you."

Chadwick was crushed with disappointment. He knew there was no way a crab could stay out of water long enough to help run a cooking school in a cornfield.

"Good luck anyway, Toulouse," Chadwick said. But as he slid back into the water and started to drift away sideways, there was a loud squawking in the air, a flutter of wings, and a splash.

"Bernie's here!" shouted Bug-Eyed Benny, always the first to see anything.

Bernie the Sea Gull was always flying off to interesting places like the United States Naval Academy in nearby Annapolis, where he sat high up on a light pole and listened to the Navy Band practice on a big green field. Sometimes, Bernie flew down into the parking lot and strutted in time to the tuba beat.

"Where are you flying in from today?" Chadwick asked. The crabs loved listening to Bernie's tales, the way little children enjoy hearing bedtime stories.

"I've just come back from Baltimore," Bernie said, shaking the water from his wings. "My, you should see what they have up there!"

"Like what?" Chadwick asked. He couldn't imagine what a big city was like.

"Well, I had a wonderful lunch for one thing," said Bernie, who loved to eat. "Today, I had two French fries and some chocolate chip cookie crumbs. It was delicious."

"Then what?" Bug-Eyed Benny asked.

"After lunch, I flew to the top of a tall building called the World Trade Center and I looked out over the harbor," said Bernie. "I even flew close to the aquarium and peeked in through the big glass windows."

Chadwick was confused. "Aquara—what?"

"Aquarium, Chadwick. You know what an aquarium is, don't you?" Bernie shook his head. He was always explaining things to the crabs.

"An aquarium is like a museum where fish and sea animals live," said Bernie. "Every year, thousands of people go to see them there and learn about how they live."

"What does the aquarium look like?" Chadwick asked.

"It's a big building with a pointed roof," said Bernie. "And at night, the aquarium is all lit up with colored lights—just like Broadway!"

"Wow!" Chadwick closed his eyes tight, imagining life in the aquarium. "I'll bet the crabs there don't have to sleep all winter!"

Chadwick had an idea. He would swim to Baltimore and live in the aquarium. That way, he wouldn't have to spend all winter napping. And, who knows? He might even become a big star!

"See you later!" Chadwick called out to his friends.

"Hey, take Orville with you," said Pincher Pete. "He's been talking up a storm this morning, and we can't get any of our packing done." All the crabs—except Chadwick—laughed. They were making fun of Orville the Oyster, who was just as quiet as a stone.

"Leave poor Orville alone," said Chadwick. "You'll hurt his feelings."

Chadwick tapped Orville's shell with a claw and told the oyster not to pay any attention to the teasing crabs.

"You're different, Orville," Chadwick said. "And I'm different too. Why, just look. All the other crabs are going to the bottom of the bay for the winter, but not me. No siree! See you later, Orville."

Chadwick swam off to get a few things together for his journey to Baltimore. Into his knapsack he put a map in case he got lost and some eel grass to snack on.

He thought about leaving a letter for Esmerelda before he left. Of all the crabs, he would miss her the most. But he decided against it, fearing that Esmerelda would find the note too soon and try to stop him from going to Baltimore.

Chadwick hoisted the little red knapsack onto his back and set off quietly. He swam and he swam. He swam until he was so tired he couldn't move. He settled onto a rock to rest and soon fell asleep.

A stream of bubbles woke Chadwick up. When he opened his eyes, he was facing a captain in the Bluefish Patrol, the police fish of the bay.

"You look lost, little crab," the bluefish said in a gruff voice. "Where are you from?"

"Shady Creek," Chadwick said, backing up and nearly falling off the rock.

"Well, you're a long way from Shady Creek."

Chadwick swallowed nervously. "I'm on my way to the aquarium in Baltimore," he said, "where I'm going to live."

"The aquarium? Ha! Ha! Ha!" the bluefish laughed. "Don't be silly. They're not going to let you live there. Not you—a common crab! You'd better listen to me and get on home."

"Oh, but *please*. I have to get to the aquarium," Chadwick pleaded.

"Come along. You're going home," the bluefish ordered.

Chadwick knew he had to obey.

*　　*　　*

Back at Shady Creek no one even noticed Chadwick had gone. As he paddled slowly through the water, wondering how he would ever get to the aquarium now, Chadwick spied Hector Spector the Jellyfish.

"Do you have any idea how I can get to Baltimore?" Chadwick asked Hector Spector.

"Oh, yes. I mean, no. Well, maybe," Hector Spector said as he changed shapes, first flat as a pancake then long like a baseball bat. Hector Spector couldn't ever make up his mind. Chadwick knew it was no use asking a jellyfish for advice.

"Thanks anyway," Chadwick said before swimming off to the marsh, where he pulled himself up onto a sandbar and put on his sunglasses. (Crabs can't stand the bright sunlight.) He thought and he thought, but he just couldn't come up with any new ideas. "I won't let go of my dream though," he said aloud.

"Oh, Chadwick! I've been looking all over for you."

Chadwick looked up to see the lovely Esmerelda with her curly crab eyelashes and dazzling red-tipped claws. She was indeed the prettiest girl crab in the bay, Chadwick thought.

"I came to help you pack," Esmerelda said. "I also want to give you my address, so you can write to me this winter." During the cold weather Esmerelda and all the girl crabs went south, to the warmer water in Virginia's part of the bay. "You will write, won't you, Chadwick?" she asked shyly.

Chadwick took off his sunglasses and looked Esmerelda in the eye. "Can you keep a secret?" he asked.

"You know I can," she said.

"Well, I'm not going to the bottom of the bay to sleep this winter. I'm going to the aquarium in Baltimore—to be a star!"

Esmerelda gasped. "What are you talking about? You belong in the water, Chadwick, not in the city!" She wasn't even sure where this Baltimore was.

"How about a game of hide and seek?" she asked, hoping that would make Chadwick forget about this silly idea of living in an aquarium.

"You're trying to change the subject," Chadwick said.

"No, I'm not. I promise you we'll talk about this aquarium business after one game."

"All right," Chadwick agreed. He loved to play hide and seek. "I'll count to ten while you hide."

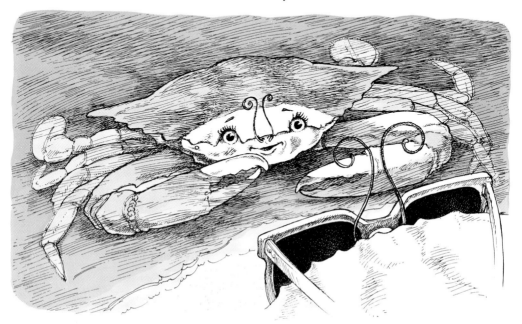

Chadwick dug himself into the sand a little and began clicking his claws. "One, two, three . . ." When he reached ten he swam off to find Esmerelda.

"She certainly found a good hiding spot this time," Chadwick said as he looked under a sunken rowboat.

Suddenly, Chadwick heard Esmerelda scream.

"Help!" she cried.

Chadwick swam as fast as he could through the water. When he saw her, she was caught in a large wire cage that was being pulled up out of the water to a boat above.

"Oh, no!" Chadwick shrieked. He knew that crabs hauled aboard boats like that one went to restaurants, where they were steamed and eaten.

Chadwick grabbed onto the edge of the cage with his claws. He wasn't about to let anything happen to Esmerelda. As long as they were together, Chadwick would find a way for them to escape.

A big man with a thick beard and shiny, black rubber gloves on his hands hauled the cage aboard a long, low workboat. The crabs blinked hard in the bright sunlight as they were dumped into a basket.

"Now, what are we going to do?" Esmerelda sobbed. "We're going to be steamed and eaten!"

Chadwick snapped his claws angrily. "No, we're not. We'll find a way out."

Meanwhile, Bernie the Sea Gull was on his favorite bell buoy with his binoculars watching the boats go by. He saw a workboat approaching and decided to fly over it in hopes of getting a handout from the watermen. Bernie never stopped thinking about food.

Just as Bernie looked down from the sky, Chadwick looked up. "Bernie! Help us! Down here on the boat!" Chadwick called out.

Bernie heard his name and swooped down low over the boat. "Oh, my goodness!" he cried. "You've been caught!"

"You've got to save us!" Chadwick hollered as the boat picked up speed. He put a claw around Esmerelda and they huddled together in the basket.

Bernie flapped his wings in confusion. "Don't worry," he squawked. "We'll get you back somehow!" He flew frantically back to Shady Creek, where he landed in a terrific splash.

"What's your hurry?" Bug-Eyed Benny asked.

"Here, here, young sea gull, you got my tail feathers all wet," Matilda fussed.

"Listen, all of you!" Bernie screeched.

Everyone gathered on the sandbar to hear what Bernie had to say.

"Chadwick and Esmerelda have been caught and are on a boat on their way to Baltimore where they'll be sold to a restaurant unless we save them."

"Not Chadwick and Esmerelda! They're the two nicest crabs in Shady Creek!" Matilda moaned.

"Immediate action is necessary!" Toulouse the Goose insisted.

"Yes, but what can we do? What can we do?" Hector Spector the Jellyfish repeated, twisting himself inside out with worry.

They all looked at each other helplessly. Matilda pulled out a handkerchief and appeared ready to faint.

Just then, a strange, deep, and gravelly voice behind them said, "I know what we can do."

Everyone was silent, wondering who had spoken.

"Who said that?" Toulouse demanded.

"I did," said the strange voice again. "I have a good idea."

They all turned to stare at Orville the Oyster's hard, wrinkled shell. Hector Spector was so surprised he froze in one shape. And Matilda fainted and fell over—plop!—right in the water.

"Orville! You've never spoken before!" exclaimed Toulouse.

"Well, that's because I never had anything to say before," said Orville. "But now I want to help Chadwick. So, listen to me." And everyone did.

"Bernie, I know you collect all kinds of things," said Orville. "Do you have anything we can use for a long ladder?"

Bernie the Sea Gull paced back and forth, thinking. "All I have are some short pieces of string and a big pile of soda can pop tops. You know, those metal tabs people pull off the tops of their sodas and carelessly throw away?"

"Great!" shouted Orville. "Go get them. We're going to build the best crab escape ladder you ever saw!"

Bernie and Toulouse flew off to get the pop tops while Bug-Eyed Benny waved Matilda's hat under her beak, trying to revive her.

When the birds returned with the metal rings Orville gave more directions. "Now, Pincher Pete, you've got the strongest claws so you bend the pop tops through one another to form a long chain. Quickly! We've got to work fast!"

The birds and crabs formed an assembly line and when they finished, Bernie coiled up the pop top ladder and draped it around Toulouse's long neck.

Orville was still giving the orders. "Toulouse, you and Bernie will fly to Baltimore and find that boat and then drop this ladder down to Chadwick and Esmerelda from the air. When they grab onto it, lift them out of the boat and they can drop back into the water."

"That's a brilliant idea," said Matilda, who was awake and sitting up now.

"Good luck!" the crabs called out, waving their claws in the air as Bernie and Toulouse flew off. Matilda held up her hat and Hector Spector was so excited he split in two!

*   *   *

It was a long flight to Baltimore from Shady Creek and by the time Bernie and Toulouse got there, they were very tired.

"I don't see them anywhere," Bernie said as they glided over the city harbor. Below them, people were walking along the waterfront at Harborplace taking pictures and eating ice cream cones. Not far away was the aquarium that Bernie had talked about. A long line of people waited to get inside.

"There's a boat coming in over there," said Bernie as he peered through his binoculars at an incoming workboat. His beak fell open. "That's the one!"

The two birds dipped and turned. When they were over the boat, they circled slowly. The sun flickered off the metal soda pop top ladder that hung around Toulouse's neck, and it caught Chadwick's eye.

"Here! We're down here!" Chadwick called out.

The birds made a daring swoop low to the boat and let one end of the ladder drop down to the crabs. Chadwick snapped onto the end of it with one claw and clutched Esmerelda with the other. Together, they were lifted from the boat into the air.

Toulouse honked in delight. Their rescue was working!

A little girl walking by on the sidewalk below pointed up and said to her mother, "Look, Mom—a sea gull, a Canada goose, and two crabs flying by in the sky!" Indeed, it was a very strange sight.

"Now, don't let go yet," Toulouse warned the crabs. "Not until we fly back over the water."

Bernie squawked happily. "Hey, Chadwick," he said. "Look below—that's the aquarium I was telling you about."

Chadwick's heart skipped a beat. "So, that's the aquarium," he said. They were almost directly above it now, and Chadwick was beginning to enjoy himself. After all, he'd never been up in the sky before and it was fun to see the world the way his bird friends did.

"Are you okay, Esmerelda?" Chadwick asked.

She nodded timidly and clung tightly to Chadwick. She was too afraid to speak or even look below.

"We'd better get back over the harbor," Bernie said to Toulouse.

But it was too late.

The weight of Chadwick and Esmerelda was too much for a ladder made from pop tops and it broke, sending the two crabs tumbling through the air. They landed with a splash in a pool outside the aquarium.

Chadwick turned to Esmerelda as they sank beneath the water. "Don't worry. We're at the aquarium. Everything is going to be fine."

But Esmerelda wasn't so sure. "There was a sign up there and it didn't say aquarium, Chadwick."

They paddled back up to the surface and peeked above the water to read the sign. "Seal Pool," Chadwick read aloud. "Well, for sure we don't have to worry now. At least it's not sharks!"

"But what's a seal?" Esmerelda wanted to know.

"A seal? Hmmm." Chadwick didn't really know. There weren't any seals in the Chesapeake Bay. "Maybe that's a seal," he said, nodding towards the big black animal swimming towards them.

"Pardon me, are you a seal?" Chadwick asked politely.

But instead of answering, the seal picked the two crabs up on its nose and tossed them way up into the air where they turned over and over and landed with a thump on the dock outside the pool.

"Quick! Over here!" Chadwick said to Esmerelda as he scrambled beneath a hot dog cart. From there, they could see the end of the dock not far away. The door to the aquarium was in the other direction.

"Come on, Chadwick, let's run for it," Esmerelda urged, eager to go home.

But Chadwick was thinking. He shook his head slowly. "No, Esmerelda," he said. "I think I'm going to stay."

Esmerelda was shocked. She didn't understand. "But, Chadwick, this is our chance!"

"Calm down and listen," Chadwick said. "This may be our chance to go back to the bay, but it's *my* chance to get inside the aquarium, where I can *be* somebody. A dream come true!"

A tear rolled down Esmerelda's face and she wiped it away with her claw. "Oh, Chadwick, I'll miss you."

"I'll be home to visit, I promise," Chadwick said as he took her two claws in his. "You go on now, quickly!"

A man was approaching and Esmerelda was scared to death of humans. She reared up on her back legs. Then, quick as a flash, she scurried to the edge of the dock. She turned once, to wave with her claw, and then jumped backwards into the water.

When Chadwick heard her splash, he knew it was his turn to run. His little legs clicked across the wooden dock and before anyone noticed he was through the door, where he jumped into the first thing he saw—a bucket near a closet.

There was water in the bucket. Chadwick sank beneath it and stayed there until closing time. Then, when it was dark, he crawled out and carefully made his way farther into the aquarium.

All around him there were huge glass tanks of fish. There were long fish and short fish, yellow fish and silver fish. There were red fish with white stripes and white fish with red stripes. There was even a sand tiger shark!

"Gosh! I've never seen so many different fish!" Chadwick said, his eyes wide with wonder. This was truly the grandest adventure he could ever imagine.

He took the escalator to the second floor and looked around there, too. Gazing up at the wide glass roof he blinked his eyes in surprise.

"Bernie! Toulouse! Hey! I see you up there! Can you see me?" Chadwick hollered at the top of his lungs.

The two birds were perched on top of the roof. Bernie was looking through his binoculars into the aquarium to make sure Chadwick was all right. They waved with their wings when they spotted Chadwick.

Although it was fun to explore the aquarium, when sunlight began to filter through the glass roof, Chadwick worried. He didn't want someone to find him and throw him back into the bay so he returned to the first floor and crawled back into the bucket to figure out his next move.

He wasn't there long before a janitor walked by. "My heavens," he said. "A crab in my cleaning pail. How in the world did you get out of your tank?" And with that, the janitor picked up the bucket and dumped Chadwick into a nearby crab exhibit, where he floated to the bottom of what was to be his happy new home.

That very same day, Chadwick showed off his sideways swimming talent to a group of school children who clapped their hands in delight. Later, he swam upside down and snapped his claws for them. They giggled when Chadwick zipped across the tank full speed.

It was the beginning of a glorious new life for Chadwick, who soon became one of the most popular attractions at the aquarium. He even had his picture in the newspaper one day. Bernie picked up a copy of the newspaper from a park bench and took it back to Shady Creek to show the others.

"I'm proud of Chadwick, my little friend," said Toulouse. "He's the first crab I've known to have his picture in the newspaper."

"That's Chadwick? It doesn't look like Chadwick," Matilda complained, squinting as she examined the picture.

"You just can't see!" Bug-Eyed Benny said, snapping the picture away with one claw. "Let me look."

Hector Spector, as usual, couldn't make up his mind whether it looked like Chadwick or not. And Orville Oyster didn't say a word.

"Oh, it's Chadwick all right," said Esmerelda, who had managed to make it safely home after a very long and exhausting swim. "And I know he's happy there. He told me that was where he wanted to be more than any place in the world."

Indeed, Chadwick loved his new life. And he was so relieved he didn't have to sleep all winter.

As for Chadwick's friends back at Shady Creek? They were happy, too, because knowing Chadwick at the aquarium was, well, like knowing a movie star.